Flowers on the Wall

Flowers on the Wall

written and illustrated by
Miriam Nerlove

MARGARET K. MCELDERRY BOOKS

This book is dedicated to the little girl from Warsaw,
who stayed in bed all winter because her apartment had no heat.
There are flowers painted on the wall behind her bed.
Her photograph, taken on the eve of the Holocaust by Roman Vishniac,
was the bittersweet inspiration for this book.

Margaret K. McElderry Books
An imprint of Simon & Schuster Children's Publishing Division
1230 Avenue of the Americas
New York, New York 10020

Book design by Ann Bobco
The text of this book is set in Janson Text.
The illustrations were rendered in watercolor.

Printed in the United States of America

First Edition

10 9 8 7 6 5 4 3 2 1

Library of Congress Cataloging-in-Publication Data
Nerlove, Miriam.
Flowers on the wall / written and illustrated by Miriam Nerlove.
p. cm.
Summary: Rachel, a young Jewish girl living in Nazi-occupied Warsaw, struggles to survive with her family and maintains hope by painting colorful flowers on her dingy apartment walls.
ISBN 0-689-50614-7
1. Jews—Persecutions—Poland—Warsaw—Juvenile fiction.
[1. Jews—Poland—Fiction. 2. Holocaust, Jewish (1939–1945)—Poland–Fiction.
3. Poland—History—Occupation, 1939–1945—Fiction.] I. Title.
PZ7.N43776F1 1995 [E]—dc20   94-31289

It was winter in Warsaw, Poland, 1938. In a small basement apartment deep inside the Jewish section of the city, Rachel lay beneath layers of blankets. She had a bad cough and had to stay in bed.

Rachel's father was at the Nalewki, the main shopping district for the Jews of Warsaw. He was searching for cloth, paper, and odds and ends to supply his dry goods store. Rachel's older brother, Nat, was with him.

"When will Papa be home?" Rachel thought longingly of the food her father might bring, especially if he made a sale or two at his store.

"Soon, soon." Her mother sighed. Mama gave Rachel some hot broth and wiped at a smudge on the window. In their dim one-room apartment, this window was important, and she kept it very clean. She sat down on the bed beside Rachel. Through the window, they guessed which neighbors the passing legs and shoes belonged to.

"Mr. Feldberg," Mama said.

"Dr. Rozensztajn," Rachel countered.

"No, it's Mr. Kramer." Mama pointed to knots in the shoelaces of the shuffling, wing-tipped shoes. "Dr. Rozensztajn would never wear broken shoelaces."

The streets began to empty; the sky was darkening. Rachel recognized her father's walk, his frayed black trousers and brown shoes, followed by a second, smaller pair of pant legs and shoes.

"Papa!" Rachel tapped on the window. "And Nat."

"Thank goodness they're home—Jews shouldn't be out so late, drawing attention to themselves!" Mama exclaimed. Rachel knew that the local police would beat a Jew for no reason if they had the opportunity. When Papa and Nat came in, Rachel saw that their hands were empty.

"It's worse than I thought," Papa said as they sat down to a dinner of hard bread and salted herring. "The boycott has hurt us terribly—Henryk usually has some goods for me to buy, but he has had no money to get new supplies. His non-Jewish customers have all been going elsewhere."

"What will we do?" Mama threw her hands up impatiently. "Jews are being forced out of their jobs—how can Jews support other Jews when none of us has any money?"

Rachel went to bed still hungry that night.

Rachel lay pressed against the wall to make room on the narrow bed for Nat. There were two beds in the apartment, one for Mama and Papa, one for Rachel and Nat. They were lucky—some families had only one bed for the whole family to sleep in.

Mama and Papa were talking softly in their bed. Rachel tried to listen, but her throat tickled and she coughed. Nat kicked her to be quiet.

"Do you hear what they're saying?" Rachel moved closer to Nat. His body was warmer than the wall.

"No, I can't hear them. And watch where you cough—you keep spitting on me!" Nat grumbled, pushing his feet against Rachel's leg. They were icy cold and Rachel cried out in protest.

"Children!" Across the room they could see Mama's dark figure sitting up. Mama and Papa had forgotten to hang the privacy sheet around their bed.

"Things are going to get much worse," Nat whispered after a few moments. "That's why Mama and Papa are worried."

"What do you mean?"

"I think Papa's going to have to close his store. We saw a lot of closed stores on our way home today—it's been going on this way for Jews for months." Nat took a deep breath. "Now go to sleep," he said. "We'll be all right. I'll bet Papa has a plan."

"A plan. What plan?" Rachel closed her eyes and thought about the day last summer when Papa had brought home a bag filled with oranges and chocolates. Maybe Papa had a good plan that would bring in more food. But Nat couldn't answer Rachel. He put his arm around her and they fell asleep.

A few days later Papa came home from work early with the bad news that Nat had predicted.

"My store's gone," he said, slumping in his chair. "Shut down like Shlomo Perl's stationery store and Nachum Polski's scrap shop. The landlord is already renting it out to a new, non-Jewish merchant."

Mama gave Papa some tea. He took a few sips and patted his coat pocket, trying to smile.

"I have a plan," Papa said, pulling out some papers. "Here are licenses—Nat and I are new members of a group of Jewish porters. Nat, you are a *tragarz*, a porter, and so am I. Maybe now we will earn some money!"

"Papa!" Rachel thought of how stooped and tired many porters looked hauling loads through the streets. These loads were meant for horses, but were more cheaply drawn by Jews. The Polish government knew that a horse needed to be fed and cared for; a Jew did not.

"Jacob!" Mama couldn't hide her disappointment.

"But what of *cheder*?" Nat loved his school and couldn't imagine not going.

"I'm sorry." Papa shook his head. "We all must work now, at least for the time being."

Rachel helped Mama in the apartment as much as she could, and every morning after Papa and Nat left, Mama put on her one good dress. She hurried to be first in line at the employment office. When the office ran out of non-Jewish girls to send to jobs, Mama would get a small job typing or sewing.

On Fridays, for Shabbos, Mama shopped at the Nalewki for vegetables, bread, and sometimes, if she had a bit more money, some meat.

"This is a little sweet, isn't it?" Papa asked one Friday night, tasting a stew Mama had cooked. He suspected they were eating slightly rancid horsemeat, which Mama had doused in a sugary sauce. Rachel and Nat thought it was delicious.

But nothing eased Rachel's loneliness. With her family gone every day, the apartment seemed smaller and grayer.

"Don't leave!" Rachel would plead with her mother in the mornings. Though her cough had gotten better, Rachel's shoes no longer fit, and there was no money to buy her new ones. She would have to stay inside all winter.

After Rachel finished scrubbing the stove in the corner, or cleaning the window, she looked at pictures in the treasured books on Mama and Papa's bookshelf. With little else to do, Rachel spent the afternoons in bed, where it was warmer. She gazed out the window, waiting for the legs of her family to pass by.

"Queen Rachel!" Nat teased, trying to cheer her up when he returned at night. Sitting on their bed with blankets covering her like woolly capes, Rachel looked like a queen on her throne.

Then one evening Papa brought home some paints and two small paintbrushes.

"They were on top of a sack in one of my loads," Papa said, handing them to Rachel. "The owner of the load said I could have them—he was an old man who told me that his eyes were going bad anyway."

Rachel fingered the soft brushes. "They're nice, Papa," she said. "But don't we need paper?"

"Paper?" Papa grinned. He waved his arm around the room. "Who needs paper?" Papa wanted to paint on the apartment's four walls instead of on paper. "This ought to liven things up!"

Right away, Papa and Rachel began painting flowers on the wall.

Now Rachel had something to do during the long, cold days. After everybody left for work, she put on thick socks and painted. Pink, purple, blue, and yellow flowers soon covered the cracked walls. They arched over the two beds, the bookshelf, and the corner kitchen, linked together by leaves and stems.

"See how I painted the petals on this one?" Rachel proudly showed Papa one evening.

"You are a wonderful artist." Papa hugged Rachel, his beard tickling her neck. Nat pointed to a deep blue flower with a round black center.

"That's my favorite," he said.

"They're lovely." Mama smiled. "I haven't seen such flowers since we visited Aunt Sophie in the country. And that was more than a year ago!"

By the time spring arrived, Rachel had used up the last of her paints. But now with the warmer weather, she could play outside in the courtyard, barefoot, with her friend Naomi. The girls squatted on the ground near Rachel's building.

"This is our feast for the ants," Naomi said, arranging some pebbles in a circle.

"Here's a roast for the queen ant." Rachel picked up a large white pebble.

"I wish we had a real roast," Naomi said. "I hate herring!"

"Me, too—hey!" Rachel jumped up.

Zev and Mark, two skinny boys from another street, kicked through the circle of pebbles and ran into an alley. Rachel and Naomi wanted to chase them, but the cobblestones hurt their feet.

A few weeks later, Papa brought home a pair of old leather shoes for Rachel. They were creased, and one had a hole in the toe, but they fit her. That same day, Mama handed Rachel a small bouquet of flowers.

"Mrs. Stasiek, the Catholic doctor's wife—she gave me these flowers when I finished sewing her blouse today," Mama said. "I want you to have them."

"They're beautiful." Rachel held the flowers to her cheek, wishing that she could paint them. Then she ran outside to show Naomi her gifts.

At last there was enough money saved for Nat to return to *cheder*. Rachel went to school for the first time, to a girls' *cheder* located in the *melamed*'s, or teacher's, apartment down the street.

"Hurry up!" Rachel yelled at Nat, even when they weren't late. He walked her to school every day, and she didn't want to miss a minute of it. Rachel was beginning to read Hebrew and Yiddish, and her class was already studying sacred Jewish texts.

Then on September 29, 1939, the Nazis occupied Warsaw. "Germans are such civilized people," Mama reassured her family. "They will treat us with respect, even though they are occupying our country."

But Mama was wrong. Life grew harder as more Jewish jobs and businesses were taken away. Warsaw Jews over the age of ten were forced to wear a white armband with a blue Star of David on it.

One evening, Papa rushed through the door, slamming it behind him.

"Naomi's father—I heard that the Germans beat him and took him away yesterday, in broad daylight. I saw them taking more Jews away today, in trucks. We must stay inside, and there will be no more *cheder* until the war's over, or until it is safer," Papa said.

Once again Rachel found herself sitting in the apartment, wrapped in blankets. She had helped Mama cover the window with a sheet, and the room was very dark. This was to keep the German soldiers outside from noticing them.

Sometimes, when Papa and Nat were out getting food, Mama carefully lifted the sheet to look for them. Sunlight hit the walls briefly, and Rachel could see that her painted flowers were beginning to fade.

"When this is all over, Papa and I will get you more paints," Mama promised, holding Rachel on her lap. She kissed Rachel's tears.

"Maybe someday we'll move to Paris," Rachel said. "My teacher says that wonderful artists live there, Mama."

But Rachel and her family never went to Paris. Instead, they were moved into the Warsaw ghetto, a part of the city that had been walled off for Jews. In July of 1942 they were deported to Treblinka, a concentration camp.

Rachel's dreams, along with those of thousands of other Warsaw
Jews, faded like the flowers on her apartment walls.
And then they were gone forever.

Note from the Author

Before the German invasion on September 29, 1939, Warsaw was a major city in Poland and a center of European Jewry. Here, during the late nineteenth and early twentieth centuries, Jews lived in poor and overcrowded conditions as shopkeepers, craftsmen, peddlers, and laborers. Anti-Semitism, a hatred toward Jewish people, was rampant, and the Jews were often persecuted by harsh laws, and ruthless police and landowners. But despite their hard lives, they had formed a way of life that was rich in intellectual activity and spiritual closeness.

Jewish communities in Warsaw, like the one in this story, were poignantly captured on film by photographers who didn't realize that the people they photographed were on the brink of destruction. Some of the most powerful pictures documenting East European Jewry between 1933 and 1939 were taken by a great photographer, the late Roman Vishniac. I was very lucky to have attended a lecture series given by Dr. Vishniac when I was a student at Pratt Institute in New York City.

Photographic records like his are an incredible gift. When the Holocaust came to an end in 1945, one-third of all the Jews in the world—six million people—had been killed in ghettos, and in death camps such as Treblinka, Auschwitz, and Birkenau. Although the people are gone, they are not forgotten, for we can look at them in these photographs and remember.

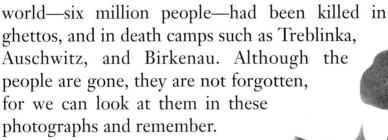